LEGO NEXO KNIGHTS™

MOVIE MAGIC

Written by Rebecca L. Schmidt

Scholastic Inc.

LEGO, the LEGO logo, NEXO KNIGHTS, the NEXO KNIGHTS logo, the Brick and Knob configurations and the Minifigure are trademarks of/ sont des marques de commerce de the LEGO Group. © 2016 The LEGO Group. All rights reserved. Produced by Scholastic Inc. under license from the LEGO Group.

Published by Scholastic Inc., Publishers since 1920. SCHOLASTIC and associated logos are trademarks and/or registered trademarks of Scholastic Inc.

ISBN 978-1-338-03802-6
10 9 8 7 6 5 4 3 2 1   16 17 18 19 20
Printed in the U.S.A.   40

First printing 2016

Lights, Camera, Action!

The NEXO KNIGHTS team was hard at work practicing in the Holo-Training Gym. Macy smiled as she swung her mace. She had grown up hearing about the adventures of great knights and heroes. Now she was one of them! Training with her fellow team members was a dream come true.

Across the gym, Lance was not as excited to train as Macy. Instead of fighting, Lance climbed on top of his weapon to get away.

"What are you doing? This isn't us training. It's you running away," Clay said, irritated.

Just then, Lance's phone began to ring. "Time-out! I call time-out!" Lance said. Clay sighed as yet another training session came to an early end.

But Lance was too excited to notice. It was his agent on the phone!

"You got the part, baby!" the agent said.

"Yes, and I so deserve it!" Lance said. He was going to be the lead actor in the new Golden Castle movie!

"I don't believe it," Axl said.

"I actually *can't* believe it," Clay said. "Merlok defeated Monstrox in the original movie, like in real history. Who would you play?"

Macy suddenly had a very bad feeling. "Oh no!" she gasped. "Please don't tell me that you—the shallowest knight ever—are playing Ned Knightly, the greatest knight there ever was!"

"Of course not," Lance said. "This film is a reimagining. A historical, art-house, sci-fi epic!"

Macy sighed. Somehow that sounded even worse than Lance playing one of her heroes.

But Lance wasn't done. "And even more great news! You can all be in it! As extras and bit players, of course."

Macy hoped that she was wrong, and that the movie would be great. But she had a bad feeling about this.

A New Evil Plan

While the knights headed to the movie set in Holo-Wood, the villains Jestro and The Book of Monsters were up to no good.

"I love the smell of destruction in the morning," Jestro said as he watched his army of monsters destroy a town. The Book of Monsters wasn't listening. He was more interested in a poster he saw on the side of a house.

"*The Golden Castle*. That brings me back to the good ol' days," he said. "I heard that Monstrox tried to take it, but Merlok and his knights stopped him."

"That's a poster for the remake of a famous movie," Jestro explained.

"I've been on a shelf for a while, remember," The Book of Monsters said. "What's a movie?"

"It's like a play projected on a screen. They film it with actors who read lines from a script," Jestro explained.

"People have to say whatever's in this 'script'?" the book asked. "Such power! We have to get this script so I can totally digest it."

"But just how are we going to be sneaky enough to do that?" Jestro asked. All the monsters he knew were much too big or loud to help.

The Book of Monsters had the perfect idea. "Summon Lavaria: super spy. Sneaky as all get out."

Jestro waved his magical staff over The Book of Monsters. "Red rover, red rover. Send Lavaria over." A huge cloud of purple magic leapt off the page and transformed into Lavaria.

"Nice to get out," she said. Jestro and The Book of Monsters smiled. With the sneaky Lavaria on their side, it was time to get this show on the road.

An Actor's Life

On the set of *The Golden Castle*, Lance was having a great time playing the hero.

"Don't fret," he said as he sent two Squirebots flying. "I, Lance Richmond, greatest of all the knights, will save the day!"

Aaron nudged Clay. It was time for Clay's line.

"Yay, verily," Clay said, rolling his eyes. "Thank Arthur Eaglewing for you because I wanted to run away. Again. Also, I wet my knight suit. Again."

Macy groaned. She couldn't believe they were being forced to say lines from such an awful script! This was exactly what she had been afraid of.

Macy's line was next, but she refused to say the terrible dialogue. "Cut, cut, cut!" the director yelled. "Read the words that my genius has approved!"

But Macy had had enough. "Never! I won't be a part of this farce!" she yelled back.
"Macy, please! Don't do it for you. Do it for me!" Lance said. But Macy just stormed off the set.

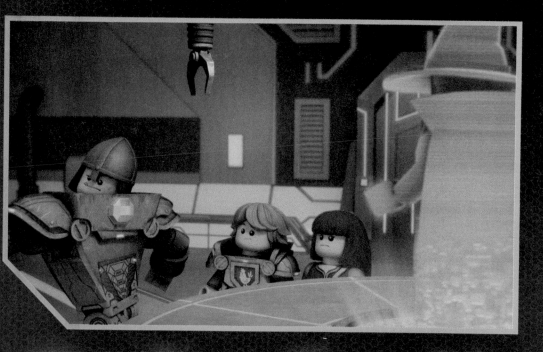

Time for an Upgrade!

While everyone was worrying about the script, Axl returned to the Fortrex to visit Merlok 2.0 and the knights-in-training, Ava and Robin.

"Axl! What are you wearing?" Merlok 2.0 asked.

"Part of my costume," Axl said, turning around to show his friends the fake upgrades on his movie outfit.

That gave Robin an idea! He could *actually* upgrade Axl's armor to make it more powerful! "I could make it hammer stuff with the force of about a thousand pounds per square inch!" Robin said, imagining all the fun possibilities.

"Oh, really?" Axl asked. "I do like to hammer!"

Robin quickly got to work. This was going to be fun!

Later that day, the NEXO KNIGHTS team was training again. But Macy wasn't enjoying it anymore. She was too angry. Her mace swept Axl off his feet, and she grabbed Aaron's shield from right beneath him. Aaron hit the ground. Hard.

"Excellent technique," Clay said as Macy struck her mace against his sword. "But you seem a little upset today, Macy. Something you'd like to talk about?"

Macy sighed. It was time to tell her friends what had really been bothering her. Macy felt different from the others: Her father, the king, didn't want her to be a real knight. And now this movie made everything she had fought so hard to be a part of look silly. "All of you are real knights, and no one can ever take that away from you." It was driving her crazy!

Nearby, in the Fortrex control room, Ava was surprised to find Robin surrounded by all the knights' shields and armor. Everything was in pieces!

"Robin, what are you doing?" Ava asked.

"Well, I decided maybe all the knights could use a boost!" Robin said.

Ava shook her head and let Robin get back to work. She just hoped that Robin could finish the upgrades before the knights needed their powers.

A Sneaky Success

Meanwhile, Lavaria had sneaked Jestro and The Book of Monsters onto the movie set. Now all they needed was to find a script for The Book of Monsters to eat. But their search was quickly interrupted when they ran into the director of the movie!

"You are supposed to be on set!" the director yelled at Lavaria, Jestro, and The Book of Monsters. He thought they were actors!

The director was not impressed with Jestro or his outfit. "I need a monster! Not some crazy half-jester."

"You, insult me?! I'll destroy you!" Jestro said. If the director wanted a monster, he'd show him a monster! He raised his staff and summoned Burnzie from The Book of Monsters. The director screamed, and his script went flying.

Now was the villains' chance! Jestro grabbed the script and fed it to The Book of Monsters. Energized by its power, monsters poured out of the evil book's pages and out onto the movie set.

Knights to the Rescue!

The knights couldn't believe their eyes. How had the evil villains sneaked past them?

"No! Jestro's going to ruin my movie! We have to stop him from destroying my career!" Lance said, running into battle.

"We have to stop them because they're monsters," said Clay, leading the rest of the knights into the fight. It was time to stop acting like knights and to actually *be* knights.

There was only one problem. Almost all of the knights were wearing costume armor and carrying fake weapons! They would need more than that to defeat Jestro and his army.

Aaron raced back to the Fortrex to get their armor from Robin.

"Axl, you're the only one in your real armor. You've got to hold them off until we get a costume change!" Lance said.

"Sure thing," Axl said, grinning.

"Filming! Keep filming!" The director pointed his camera at the battle. This was just what he needed for his movie!

There were monsters everywhere, full of the power from the director's script. Axl tried his best to fight

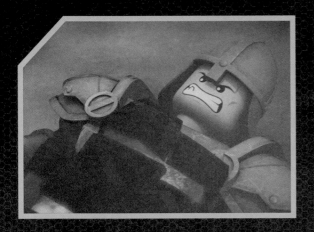

them, but he was only one knight. Soon he was buried under Burnzie and a horde of monsters.

Just in time, Aaron flew back into the battle with everyone's armor and weapons. Now the team could end this!

"Time to try out this new Ultra Armor!" Axl said. He couldn't wait to use Robin's upgrades.

"Merlok! NEXOOOOO Knight!" Clay yelled.

Costume Change!

Merlok's voice filled the set. "NEXO Power: Ultra Armor Activate!"

Suddenly, Clay's armor now had bonus whirling swords, and Lance's armor grew an awesome set of wings! Axl's giant fists gave him even more ways to pound his enemies into the ground. Aaron had four cannons of firepower to use. And Macy? Macy had a Mace Blaster!

"Charge!" Macy screamed as she ran toward the monsters. These new upgrades were awesome!

"How exactly do these things . . ." Lance began to say, but before he could finish his sentence his new wings opened and flew him high up into the air! "Whoa!!!" Lance yelled. He didn't know how to control his new armor yet!

Luckily, everyone else was learning fast. Aaron's cannons were destroying monsters all around him. Macy used her Mace Blaster to take down Burnzie in one shot!

Lance finally got his feet back on the ground, and his wings worked great with Clay's new swords to create a tornado of destruction against the monsters! Axl's new iron fists were pounding monsters left and right!

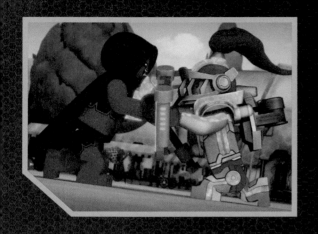

Macy noticed Lavaria trying to creep away from the battle. Not on her watch! She ran at the monster, but the sneaky spy pushed her away.

Aaron flew past, distracting Lavaria just long enough for Macy to bring out her Mace Blaster. It was time for her to save the day, just like all the knights that had inspired her.

"You're out of the picture!" she told Lavaria as she fired.

Jestro and The Book of Monsters knew they were defeated. It was time for them to escape before the NEXO KNIGHTS team caught them!

"Well, guys," Macy said. "I think that's a wrap."

But as the knights celebrated their victory, the director couldn't believe his eyes! "My beautiful set! My epic film! Ruined!" What was going to happen to *The Golden Castle* remake now?

Let's Go to the Movies!

A few weeks later, Robin, Ava, and the knights all attended the premiere of *The Golden Castle*. "Everyone, settle down. This is a momentous occasion for you, so you don't want to miss a word!" Lance said. He was so excited to see himself playing a dashing hero on-screen!

But when the movie started, it wasn't the movie Lance had thought it was! It was all of his worst mistakes from the set! The director had edited the movie to make Macy the hero! It even included her epic takedown of Lavaria.

Everyone in the audience burst into laughter as they watched Lance lose control of his new wings.

"Lance, I didn't think this movie was a good idea at first, but thank you so much for letting me be a part of it," Macy said.

"We need to talk. I can make you a star!" Lance's old agent told Macy.

"I'm more interested in battling monsters," Macy said. After all, she was living her dream of being a knight. That was so much cooler than just playing one in a movie. And no one could take that away from her.

Dear Family and Friends of New Readers,

Welcome to Scholastic Reader. We have taken over ninety years' worth of experience with teachers, parents, and children and put it into a program that is designed to match your child's interest and skills. Each Scholastic Reader is designed to support your child's efforts to learn how to read at every age and every stage.

LEVEL PRE1
- First Reader
- Preschool – Kindergarten
- ABC's
- First words

LEVEL 1
- Beginning Reader
- Preschool – Grade 1
- Sight words
- Words t~~o~~ ~~~~

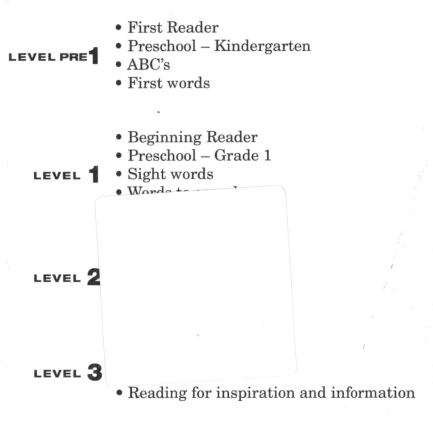

LEVEL 2

LEVEL 3
- Reading for inspiration and information

For ideas about sharing books with your new reader, please visit www.scholastic.com. Enjoy helping your child learn to read and love to read!

Happy Reading!

— Scholastic Inc.

YOU OUGHTA BE I[N PICTURES]

When a famous Holo-Wood director asks Lance to star in his latest movie, the knight is ready for his close-up! Lance even invites his NEXO KNIGHTS™ friends to be in the movie, too. But when the cameras start rolling, Lance doesn't want to share the spotlight. Will Lance's ego ruin the movie . . . and his friendships?

 LEGO® NEXO KNIGHTS™: MERLOK 2.0

 Download the free app!
LEGO.COM/devicecheck

 1
2

 LEGO, the LEGO logo, NEXO KNIGHTS, the NEXO KNIGHTS logo, the Brick and Knob configurations and the Minifigure are trademarks of/ sont des marques de commerce de the LEGO Group. © 2016 The LEGO Group. All rights reserved. Produced by Scholastic Inc. under license from the LEGO Group.

$3.99 US $5.50 CAN

ISBN 978-1-338-03802-6

50399

EAN

9 781338 038026